A Christmas Gift
from God

SHARON KIZZIAH-HOLMES

Paperback-Press
an imprint of A & S Publishing
A & S Holmes, Inc.

ISBN - 10: 1-945669-14-4
ISBN - 13: 978-1-945669-14-9

ACKNOWLEDGMENTS

Thanks to my husband for always supporting my writing and everything I do. Thanks for letting me take off for weekend retreats, for letting me sit for hours in my office, but most of all thanks for loving me.

CHAPTER 1

Keli held onto the brown paper bag as she placed the key in the door lock and turned it. It was hard enough to carry groceries in when there was snow on the ground, contending with her big belly only made the plight worse.

She glanced at the Christmas carolers a couple of doors down. Their voices were beautiful, but she felt far from festive. "Bah, humbug."

She pushed the door open then entered the warm coziness of her kitchen. With a deep sigh she set the sack on the table. It was good to be home. Even if the place hadn't been the happiest on earth the last couple of years.

Her baby was due in three weeks. Going to

town had never been a problem before, but now it seemed too much like a chore. What would it be like after the child came? It would be her luck to go into labor on Christmas day and ruin everyone's holiday.

Why had she let this happen? The responsibility of a little one was the last thing she wanted. If she and Mark were getting along better, having a baby would be a joyous occasion.

She glanced at the clock. He would be home soon. She hoped he was in a good mood. Doubt pressed her, forcing out another sigh.

Placing the items she'd bought at the store in the cabinet, she prayed for things to get better. She wouldn't have stayed with her husband if she didn't love him. Deep down inside Mark was a good man, but it seemed he lacked the gift of *commitment* to anything but his job.

Their first year together was wonderful. Every day like a honeymoon she'd never forget. They had talked about buying Colliers General Store, a nice little country grocery with a great living area above it and a wonderful, fenced, park-like yard in the back. It was their dream and she'd wanted it more than anything, but when Mark got his promotion to CEO of the local division of the company, his attention and his disposition shifted.

It seemed she couldn't do a thing to lighten

his burden, nor did she feel he wanted her to. Finally, about a year ago, aware her dream would never come true, she stopped talking about Colliers and tried not to think about it. It broke her heart, but she couldn't take the bickering anymore.

Now, they hardly spoke, and she hated life without him. Her loneliness was often overwhelming. She wanted him back so badly.

Then, as if to punctuate their detachment, the one night in the last twelve months they'd made love, if she could call it that, she'd gotten pregnant and Mark didn't seem to care.

CHAPTER 2

Blinking lights on the Christmas tree stole her stare and the voices of the carolers drifted in from outdoors. It would be rude to ignore them, so she opened the door and stood to listen then Mark pulled into the drive.

Her heart plummeted when he got out of the car. He had been so handsome once. Tall, dark and handsome she used to call him. Now, that once good-looking face held an incomprehensible gloom. It seemed it was in his heart, his soul as well. She only wished he'd quit that job. Her heart broke for him, but mostly for them and their child.

The carolers' voices rang through the air as she watched her husband make his way to the porch. *God, I love that man. Please bring him back to me. I pray we find our way back to the happy life we once knew. It seems only You can do that.*

"...Hark the herald angels sing, glory to the new born king..."

"Hi,"

"Hi, Mark." She was surprised when he took a place beside her and slipped his arm around her waist. Was it just for show? Were the carolers' words getting to him? Maybe her prayer was heard and God had already touched something inside him. Why analyze the situation? She just wanted to enjoy the rare moment.

"...Silent night, holy night, all is calm all is bright, round..."

"Sing along folks," said one of the vocalists. "...Jingle bells, jingle bells, jingle all the way. Oh what fun..."

To Keli's amazement, she heard Mark's deep voice singing the words to the song.

Mark smiled down at her and continued to sing. "...it is to ride in a one horse open sleigh. Hey! Jingle bells, jingle bells..."

What had gotten into him? She didn't care; if he'd only stay this way. Snuggling into his embrace she reveled in his warmth. Oh how she'd missed his touch, his love, him. *Thank you for this moment, Lord.*

Sorrow passed through her heart when

Mark and the choir finished their songs. She didn't want it to be over, not yet, but the well wishes of the people leaving the yard were exactly the things she prayed for over the last few months.

"Happy Holidays."

"Merry Christmas."

"God be with you."

A small boy took the steps and stopped in front of her and Mark. His eyes were so sweet, and he seemed to have an aura about him. Something special.

"Are you going to have a baby?"

She glanced at Mark. His eyes were focused on the child. She turned her attention back to the boy. "Why, yes, we are."

He gazed at her then at Mark. "Are you going to love it like my mommy and daddy love me?"

The lump in her throat went down hard when Mark's arm dropped from her waist. She missed the warmth of his embrace. "I hope so," she replied.

"Good. My mommy says children are a gift from God and should be cherished. She says love is something some folks never know." He smiled from ear to ear. "I'm glad you two love each other. It makes me feel good."

He jumped from the steps then turned back toward them. "Hey, did you know the baby Jesus was born on Christmas Day?"

"Really?" Kelly replied.

"Yep. Jesus was God's gift to all of us."

A woman shouted form the crowd. "Jessie, come on, honey."

"I gotta go now." His hand flew into the air with a wave. "Merry Christmas! And happy birthday to baby Jesus."

They watched the carolers move to the next block, then silently she followed her husband into the house. The little boy was right, this child was a gift from God, but she could see from the look on Mark's face that the boy's words hadn't changed his attitude. He didn't speak a word as he loosened his tie and went into the bedroom to change clothes.

Hopelessness crept into her being. Then, though it seemed impossible, a silent voice spoke to her heart.

"For your baby's sake, be at peace."

"I only wish it were that simple," she whispered to thin air and wondered if she was going crazy.

"Peace is within you. Embrace it, my child."

She felt the words more than heard them. Warmth encircled her and she looked down, rubbed her swollen stomach, and calm flowed through her.

What had just happened? Tears welled in her eyes and joy filled her heart when she realized, for the first time, she was happy about her pregnancy.

CHAPTER 3

When Keli entered her mother's house on Christmas morning, the aroma of baking turkey, pumpkin pie and homemade rolls tantalized her senses. The familiar smells wafted across the air of her childhood home just as they did every holiday season of her life. A smile touched the corners of her mother's mouth and the older woman's face brightened. She loved her mom so much.

"Hi, Kel." The woman put her arms around her daughter. "I'm so glad you're here. Where's Mark?"

Pain stabbed her soul, but the subject couldn't be avoided. She backed away from her mother's embrace and met her mother's gaze.

"Keli?"

"I'm not sure where he is, Mom. Anymore, it's like that more than not. He said he had to go out of town. That job has taken over his life, and mine, but I'm okay with it." She wasn't really okay with it, but since her calming experience she handled things better. It was clear God's hand was leading her through her disappointment.

"Surely he's not working on Christmas Day," her mother said while stirring the fruit salad.

"He told me he'd be home yesterday, but never showed. He doesn't seem to care anymore and I try not to worry but..."

Her mother smiled, shook her head and put the fruit salad in the fridge. "Maybe he has a wonderful Christmas surprise he's working on for you. You never know."

The pressure on her back almost unbearable, she had to sit down. She'd been having strange feelings all day. She hung her head and added, "He didn't even call, Mom."

"I hope he didn't have an accident." Concern wrote a wrinkled path across her mother's forehead.

"He didn't have an accident. I would have heard from the authorities by now. I don't think he wants to be around me. I'm afraid I may have to raise this child on my own."

"Oh, Keli, what are you saying? Mark loves

you. I know that for a fact."

How could her mother think that after the way he'd been acting? "He used to. But now?"

Wiping her hands on her apron, her mom said, "Don't be ridiculous. He loves you and he'll be here. You wait and see."

Hoping above all hope she was right, but fearing she wasn't, Keli stood. "Let's not talk about it. We'd better get things done around here before everyone shows up."

She took two steps toward the sink and felt a trickle of water on her leg. It quickly turned into a gush. "Oh, no!" Pain pierced her stomach and back.

Her mother rushed to her side. "What is it, honey?"

"My water broke." She accepted the older woman's gentle help back to the chair. She was afraid this would happen. "Why today, of all days?"

"Let me get your dad." Her mom smiled and took off her apron. "We have plenty of time. The first one usually takes a while to come. You just sit here. I'll be right back. Everything's going to be okay."

"But what about Christmas dinner? Everyone will be here soon."

"Not, don't you worry about that. I'll call your sister and have her call the others. Christmas is the perfect day to have my first grandchild." She turned and walked out of the room.

Her Mom's encouraging words did little to ease her concern. Another pain grabbed Keli's back and squeezed forward like a giant hand pressing her belly. It lasted a short time then let up.

Her mind drifted to her husband. What had it mattered that he wouldn't take the Lamaze classes with her? He wasn't here to help her anyway. Somehow she knew it would be like this.

Distress hit her in a sinking condemnation. The contractions were too strong and far too close together. At least she knew that much. Her pulse threatened to run away with itself. She had to get to the hospital before the baby came right here at the house. "Mom, Dad, hurry!"

CHAPTER 4

The epidural brought blessed relief from the hard and fast contractions. The doctor indicated they were lucky to have gotten to the hospital as quickly as they did. She only wished Mark was there.

"Your Christmas baby's about to be born, Mrs. Williams," said one of the nurses.

Christmas baby her foot! She just wanted the pressure to stop.

The doctor's voice was light-hearted. "Push Keli, push. Just a couple more times and it will be over."

She bore down with all her might. Where the hell was Mark?! She'd like to break his neck for putting her through this. "Men!" she yelled as the contraction let up.

The doctor leaned back a little. "You can stop pushing now, but only for a moment. We're almost there."

We're almost there? He wasn't doing anything but sitting there watching her do all the work. The room was full of people, but somehow she felt all alone. *God, please do something.*

There was a knock at the door of her labor and delivery room. A nurse approached it. "May I help you?" she asked through the hard wood.

"I'm Mrs. William's husband. May I come in, please?" came a deep voice from the other side.

The delivery room door opened. She raised her head and recognized Mark's tall frame. She was never so glad to see him, even if she did hate him at the moment. Her words were more harsh than she'd intended. "Did you decide to show up?" She felt her stomach knot once again and heard the doctor speak.

"Push, Keli. We're almost there. Push."

Mark rushed to her side and took her hand. "I'm sorry, honey. I had some business to take care of, but I'm here now."

Business. Business was always the first thing on his list. "Well, if you'll excuse me," she said between gasping breaths, "I have some business to take care of right now." With all her might, she bore down.

"This is it!" The doctor leaned forward. "Don't stop now, there's the head."

Mark's touch was comforting as he wiped a piece of sweat-drenched hair away from her brow. She almost felt as if he cared. After a few short breaths she bore down as hard as she could.

"Here it comes, folks. Press Keli, you're doing great. The head is out now give me one more good push."

With Mark's help, she rose up a little and gave it all she had. She felt her face contort with the strain, the pressure almost unbearable. "Aaaahhhhhh!"

The tension in her abdomen was suddenly gone. She fell back against the bed, breathing in short sporadic spurts. Again, she felt Mark's touch on her face. She forced herself to look into his dark brown eyes. Was that a smile she saw in them?

He glanced at the newborn then back at her. "We have a boy, honey."

The baby's cry filled her ears. What a beautiful sound. "A boy?"

"That's right. Our son."

She hadn't seen that look in Mark's eyes in a long time. The look of happiness. Could it be he'd changed overnight? Doubtful. She wouldn't allow herself to get her hopes up, but she *would* let herself enjoy this flash of joy.

Only minutes had passed, though it seemed like hours. Exhaustion turned her body into a weakened mass but when the nurse brought the tiny infant in her fatigue was all but gone. The woman laid the child on Keli's chest."

"Here's your son, Mrs. Williams."

The tiny bundle in her arms drew unstoppable tears of joy. She never imagined it would be like this. So much love. She pulled the blanket back from his face and smiled. "Look, Mark. He's got your nose." When she glanced up at her husband, she saw tears in his eyes.

"He truly is a gift from God, isn't he?"

She met his gaze. "Yes, he is."

Mark knelt beside her. His features looked almost peaceful. Where had he been last night? She could almost forgive him anything if he, the real Mark, would find his way back to her.

She reached out and touched his beard-stubbled cheek. God, she'd missed him. "Mark, I–"

"Wait, don't say a word. I have to give you something before we talk." He reached into his shirt pocket, pulled out some papers and handed them to her.

Was he divorcing her? So quickly after such a beautiful experience he'd do this?

CHAPTER 5

She closed her eyes for only a moment then Mark's voice came through her thoughts.

"You've just given me a wonderful gift. What's in those papers is for you, for us, all three of us. I love you, Kel."

He loved her? Did he just say he loved her?

A nurse approached the bed. "I need to take your baby away for a while and get him all cleaned up and weighed. I'll bring him back as soon as I can."

Keli nodded, gently kissed her son's forehead than gave him to the lady in white. "Bye, bye, sweet baby. See you soon."

She watched the woman leave the room then turned her attention back to the papers

Mark had given her. "What is this?" His eyes sparkled with mischief, a little of the old Mark again. It couldn't be divorce papers. He said he loved her.

"Open it and find out."

Slowly, she unfolded the document. Her worst fear, that it was divorce papers, had passed. She scanned the pages and her pulse raced faster with every word. At the bottom of the last page, she saw his signature. "Mark! You didn't!" His smile broadened into a toothy grin. He almost looked like his old self.

"Yep. I did."

He bent and she accepted his ever-so-gentle kiss. "Really?"

"Really, sweetheart. I quit my job and now Colliers General Store belongs to the Williams family."

"I don't believe it." The feeling of love washed through her and overpowered any doubts or discomfort she had. She threw her arms around his neck. His embrace was something she hadn't forgotten.

"That's where I've been for the last few days. Getting things ready so when you leave the hospital, we can go directly there and move right in."

"But I haven't packed or anything."

"Don't worry about it. The Colliers are gone and tomorrow the movers are going to take care of everything for us."

"Oh, sweetheart, you're wonderful." *Thank you, God. Thank you for answering my prayers.*

"And guess what. I fixed up the nursery myself."

"You did?"

"Yep. I got with your mother and she told me all the things you wanted."

"So she was in on this and didn't tell me? That's why she didn't give me a baby shower and said you might be working on a Christmas present for me." She glanced at her mom and dad who had entered the room only moments before. "You sneak!"

Her mom stepped forward and gave her a hug. "See, I told you he loves you."

The hospital door squeaked open and the nurse brought the baby back to the bedside. "Here you go. A perfect little man."

Keli watched as Mark took the blanketed bundle from the woman. His face beamed like a new father's should. He laid the baby next to her and leaned close.

"What are we going to name this Christmas gift from God?"

She couldn't believe they hadn't even talked about a name. Her thoughts went back to the little boy who'd been with the Christmas carolers that day a few weeks ago. "How about Jessie?"

He smiled. "Jessie. I remember him well. He was the young man who finally made me see the light. When he said that children are a gift from God, and that some people never know love, I realized what I'd been putting you through." He kissed her lips then the cheek of their son. "Can you forgive me, Kel?"

Her love for her handsome husband soared. She quoted more of Jessie's words, "Hey, did you know that the baby Jesus was born on Christmas Day?"

Mark threw his head back in laughter. "And so was our baby Jessie. Thank God for His gift to all of us."

ABOUT THE AUTHOR

I live in the beautiful Ozarks with my husband and two dogs. I have seventeen grandkids and four great grands and one on the way know... =) However, I love each and every one of them with all my heart, and wouldn't change a thing.

My interest in writing novels came in the early 1990's. A friend suggested we write a book together, so I took her up on it. I joined Ozarks Romance Authors and a whole new world opened up for me. I'm now a member of many other writing groups. I absolutely love writing, editing, publishing and teaching the basics of writing to others.

Hubby and I are retired road musicians. We have a boutique recording studio in our home and record everything from karaoke singles and live bands, to audio books.

I have an indie author publishing company, Paperback-Press, and love helping others get their writing published.

Keli's story came to me in a dream and I had to get it down on paper. I love this sweet story and hope you enjoy it, too.

OTHER PUBLICATIONS
by
Sharon Kizziah-Holmes

The Will and the Wisp
Ride the Storm
Romantic Short Stories
Gamble for Life
Paranormal Short Stories
A Star That Twinkled
A Dogs Life